Munschworks 2
The Second Munsch Treasury

Munschworks 2
The Second Munsch Treasury

stories by Robert Munsch
illustrations by
Michael Martchenko and Hélène Desputeaux

Annick Press Ltd.
Toronto • New York • Vancouver

Sixth printing, July 2006

We acknowledge the support of the Canada Council for the Arts, the Ontario Arts Council, and the Government of Canada through the Book Publishing Industry Development Program (BPIDP) for our publishing activities.

Cataloging in Publication Data

Munsch, Robert N., 1945-
        Munschworks 2

ISBN 1-55037-553-9

I. Desputeaux, Hélène. II. Martchenko, Michael. III. Title. IV. Title: Munschworks two.

PS8576.U575M86 1999   jC813.'54   C99-930523-9
PZ7.M927Mu 1999

The art in this book was rendered in watercolor.
The text was typeset in Century Oldstyle and Adlib.

Distributed in Canada by: Published in the U.S.A. by Annick Press (U.S.) Ltd.
Firefly Books Ltd.   Distributed in the U.S.A. by:
66 Leek Crescent   Firefly Books (U.S.) Inc.
Richmond Hill, ON   P.O. Box 1338
L4B 1H1   Ellicott Station
                                   Buffalo, NY 14205

Printed and bound in China.

visit us at: **www.annickpress.com**

Contents

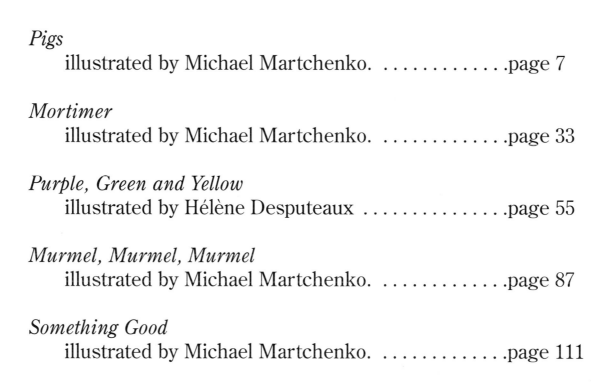

Pigs

by Robert Munsch
illustrated by
Michael Martchenko

Megan's father asked her to feed the pigs on her way to school. He said, "Megan, please feed the pigs, but don't open the gate. Pigs are smarter than you think. Don't open the gate."

"Right," said Megan. "I will not open the gate. Not me. No sir. No, no, no, no, no."

So Megan went to the pig pen. She looked
at the pigs. The pigs looked at Megan.

Megan said, "These are the dumbest-look-
ing animals I have ever seen. They stand
there like lumps on a bump. They wouldn't do
anything if I did open the gate." So Megan
opened the gate just a little bit. The pigs stood
there and looked at Megan. They didn't do
anything.

Megan said, "These are the dumbest-look-
ing animals I have ever seen. They stand
there like lumps on a bump. They wouldn't
even go out the door if the house was on fire."
So Megan opened the gate a little bit more.
The pigs stood there and looked at Megan.
They didn't do anything.

Then Megan yelled, "HEY YOU DUMB PIGS!" The pigs jumped up and ran right over Megan, WAP—WAP—WAP—WAP—WAP, and out the gate.

When Megan got up she couldn't see the pigs anywhere. She said, "Uh-oh, I am in bad trouble. Maybe pigs are not so dumb after all." Then she went to tell her father the bad news. When she got to the house Megan heard a noise coming from the kitchen. It went, "OINK, OINK, OINK."

"That doesn't sound like my mother. That doesn't sound like my father. That sounds like pigs."

She looked in the window. There was her father, sitting at the breakfast table. A pig was drinking his coffee. A pig was eating his newspaper. And a pig was peeing on his shoe.

"Megan," yelled her father, "you opened the gate. Get these pigs out of here."

Megan opened the front door a little bit. The pigs stood and looked at Megan. Finally Megan opened the front door all the way and yelled, "HEY YOU DUMB PIGS!" The pigs jumped up and ran right over Megan, WAP—WAP—WAP—WAP—WAP, and out the door.

Megan ran outside, chased all the pigs into the pig pen and shut the gate. Then she looked at the pigs and said, "You are still dumb, like lumps on a bump." Then she ran off to school. Just as she was about to open the front door, she heard a sound: "OINK, OINK, OINK."

She said, "That doesn't sound like my
teacher. That doesn't sound like the principal.
That sounds like pigs."

Megan looked in the principal's window.
There was a pig drinking the principal's coffee.
A pig was eating the principal's newspaper.
And a pig was peeing on the principal's shoe.
The principal yelled, "Megan, get these pigs
out of here!"

Megan opened the front door of the school a
little bit. The pigs didn't do anything. She
opened the door a little bit more. The pigs still
didn't do anything. She opened the door all the
way and yelled, "HEY YOU DUMB PIGS!"
The pigs jumped up and ran right over Megan,
WAP—WAP—WAP—WAP—WAP, and out
the door.

Megan went into the school. She sat down
at her desk and said, "That's that! I finally got
rid of all the pigs." Then she heard a noise:
"OINK, OINK, OINK." Megan opened her
desk, and there was a new baby pig. The
teacher said, "Megan! Get that dumb pig out
of here!"

Megan said, "Dumb? Who ever said pigs were dumb? Pigs are smart. I am going to keep it for a pet."

At the end of the day the school bus finally came. Megan walked up to the door, then heard something say, "OINK, OINK, OINK."

Megan said, "That doesn't sound like the bus driver. That sounds like a pig." She climbed up the stairs and looked in the bus. There was a pig driving the bus, pigs eating the seats and pigs lying in the aisle.

A pig shut the door and drove the bus down the road.

It drove the bus all the way to Megan's farm, through the barnyard and right into the pig pen.

Megan got out of the bus, walked across the barnyard and marched into the kitchen. She said, "The pigs are all back in the pig pen. They came back by themselves. Pigs are smarter than you think."

And Megan never let out any more animals.

At least, not any more pigs.

Mortimer

by Robert Munsch
illustrated by
Michael Martchenko

One night Mortimer's mother took him upstairs to go to bed—

thump thump thump thump thump thump thump.

When they got upstairs Mortimer's mother opened the door to his room.

She threw him into bed and said,

"MORTIMER, BE QUIET."

Mortimer shook his head, yes.

The mother shut the door.
Then she went back down the stairs—
thump _{thump}_{thump}_{thump}_{thump.}

As soon as she got back downstairs
Mortimer sang,

    Clang, clang, rattle-bing-bang
    Gonna make my noise all day.
    Clang, clang, rattle-bing-bang
    Gonna make my noise all day.

Mortimer's father heard all that noise. He came up the stairs—

thump thump thump thump thump thump.

He opened the door and yelled,

"MORTIMER, BE QUIET."

Mortimer shook his head, yes.

The father went back down the stairs—
thump
thump
thump
thump
thump.

As soon as he got to the bottom of the stairs Mortimer sang,

Clang, clang, rattle-bing-bang
Gonna make my noise all day.
Clang, clang, rattle-bing-bang
Gonna make my noise all day.

All of Mortimer's seventeen brothers and
sisters heard that noise, and they all came
up the stairs—

thump
thump
thump
thump
thump
thump.

They opened the door and yelled in a
tremendous, loud voice,

"MORTIMER, BE QUIET."

Mortimer shook his head, yes.

The brothers and sisters shut the door
and went downstairs—
thump
thump
thump
thump
thump.

As soon as they got to the bottom of the
stairs Mortimer sang,

Clang, clang, rattle-bing-bang
Gonna make my noise all day.
Clang, clang, rattle-bing-bang
Gonna make my noise all day.

They got so upset that they called the police. Two policemen came and they walked very slowly up the stairs—

thump^{thump}thump^{thump}^{thump}^{thump.}

They opened the door and said in very deep, policemen-type voices,

"MORTIMER, BE QUIET."

The policemen shut the door and went
back down the stairs—
thump thump thump thump thump.

As soon as they got to the bottom of the
stairs Mortimer sang,

Clang, clang, rattle-bing-bang
Gonna make my noise all day.
Clang, clang, rattle-bing-bang
Gonna make my noise all day.

Well, downstairs no one knew what to do.
The mother got into a big fight with the policemen.
The father got into a big fight with the brothers and sisters.

Upstairs, Mortimer got so tired waiting for someone to come up that he fell asleep.

Purple,
Green
and
Yellow

by Robert Munsch
illustrated by
Hélène Desputeaux

Brigid went to her mother and said, "I need some coloring markers. All my friends have coloring markers. They draw wonderful pictures. Mommy, I need some coloring markers."

"Oh, no!" said her mother. "I've heard about those coloring markers. Kids draw on walls, they draw on the floor, they draw on themselves. You can't have any coloring markers."

"Well," said Brigid, "there are these new coloring markers. They wash off with just water. I can't get into any trouble with coloring markers that wash off. Get me some of those."

"Well," said her mother, "all right."

So her mother went out and got Brigid 500 washable coloring markers.

Brigid went up to her room and drew wonderful pictures. She drew lemons that were yellower than lemons, and roses that were redder than roses, and oranges that were oranger than oranges.

Her mother was amazed. She said,
"Wow! My kid is an artist."

But after a week Brigid got bored. She went to her mother and said, "Mom, did I draw on the wall?"

"Nnnnooo," said her mother.
"Did I draw on the floor?"
"Nnnnooo," said her mother.
"Did I draw on myself?"
"Nnnnooo," said her mother.

"Well," said Brigid, "I didn't get into any trouble and I need some new coloring markers. All my friends have them. Mommy, there are coloring markers that smell. They have ones that smell like roses and lemons and oranges and even ones that smell like cow plops. Mom, they have coloring markers that smell like any- thing you want! Mom, I need those coloring markers."

Her mother went out and got 500 coloring markers that smelled. Then Brigid went upstairs and she drew pictures. She drew lemons that smelled like lemons, and roses that smelled like roses, and oranges that smelled like oranges, and cow plops that smelled like cow plops.

Her mother said, "Wow! My kid is an artist."

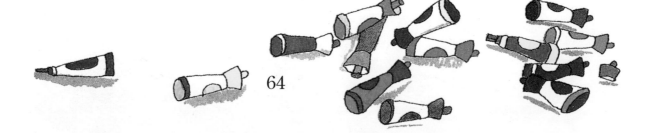

64

But after a week Brigid got bored. She said, "Mom, did I draw on the floor?"

"Nnnnooo," said her mother.

"Did I draw on the walls?"

"Nnnnooo," said her mother.

"Did I draw on myself?"

"Nnnnooo," said her mother.

"Well," said Brigid, "I need some new coloring markers. These are the best kind. All my friends have them. They are super-indelible-never-come-off-till-you're-dead-and-maybe-even-later coloring markers. Mom, I need them."

So her mother went out and got 500 super-indelible-never-come-off-till-you're-dead-and-maybe-even-later coloring markers. Brigid took them and drew pictures for three weeks. She drew lemons that looked better than lemons, and roses that looked better than roses and oranges that looked better than oranges and sunsets that looked better than sunsets.

Then she got bored.

She said, "I'm tired of drawing on the paper. But I am not going to draw on the walls and I am not going to draw on the floor and I'm not going to draw on myself —but everybody knows it's okay to color your finger-nails. Even my mother colors her fingernails."

So Brigid took a purple super-indelible-never-come-off-till-you're-dead-and-maybe-even-later coloring marker, and she colored her thumbnail bright purple.

And that was so pretty, she colored all her fingernails purple, black and yellow.

And that was so pretty, she colored her hands yellow, green and red.

69

And that was so pretty, she colored her face purple, green, yellow and blue.

And that was so pretty, she colored her belly-button blue.

And that was so pretty, she colored herself all sorts of colors almost entirely all over.

Then Brigid looked in the mirror and said, "What have I done! My mother is going to kill me." So she ran into the bathroom and washed her hands for half an hour. Nothing came off. Her hands still looked like mixed-up rainbows.

Then she had a wonderful idea.

She reached way down into the bottom of the coloring markers and got a special-colored marker. It was the same color she was. She took that marker and colored herself all over until she was her regular color again. In fact, she looked even better than before—almost too good to be true.

She went downstairs and her mother said, "Why, Brigid, you're looking really good today."

"Right," said Brigid.

Then her mother said, "It's time to wash your hands for dinner."

But Brigid was afraid that the special color would not stick to the colors underneath, so she said, "I already washed my hands."

But her mother smelled her hands and said, "Ahhh. No soap!" She took Brigid into the bathroom and washed her hands and face. All the special color came off and Brigid looked like mixed-up rainbows.

"Oh, no!" said her mother. "Brigid, did you color your hands with the coloring markers that wash off?"

"Nnnnooo."

"Brigid, did you color your hands with the coloring markers that smell?"

"Nnnnnooooo."

"Did you use the super-indelible-never-come-off-till-you're-dead-and-maybe-even-later coloring markers?"

"Yes!"

"Yikes!" yelled her mother.

She called the doctor and said, "HELP! HELP! HELP! My daughter has colored herself with super-indelible-never-come-off-till-you're-dead-and-maybe-even-later coloring markers."

"Oh, dear," said the doctor. "Sometimes they never come off."

The doctor came over and gave Brigid a large, orange pill. She said, "Take this pill, wait five minutes and then take a bath."

So Brigid took the pill, waited five minutes, and jumped into the bathtub. Her mother stood outside the door and yelled, "Is it working? Is it working?"

"Yes," said Brigid. "Everything is coming off." And Brigid was right, everything had come off. When Brigid walked out of the bathroom she was invisible.

"Oh, no," yelled her mother. "You can't go to school if you're invisible. You can't go to university if you're invisible. You'll never get a job if you're invisible. Brigid, you've wrecked your life!"

"Don't worry," said Brigid. She ran into her room, got the special-colored marker and colored herself entirely all over until you couldn't tell the difference. In fact, she looked even better than before — almost too good to be true.

But her mother said, "Brigid, you can't go through life like that. You're just a picture. Everyone will know there is something wrong."

"No they won't," said Brigid.

"Yes they will," said her mother.

"No they won't," said Brigid. "I colored Daddy while he was taking a nap and you haven't noticed anything yet!"

"Good heavens!" yelled her mother, and she ran into the living-room and looked at Daddy. He looked even better than before—almost too good to be true.

"Doesn't he look great?" asked Brigid.

"I couldn't even tell the difference," said her mother.

"Right," said Brigid, "and neither will he...

As long as he doesn't get wet."

Murmel, Murmel, Murmel

by Robert Munsch
illustrated by
Michael Martchenko

When Robin went out into her back yard, there was a large hole right in the middle of her sandbox. She knelt down beside it and yelled, "ANYBODY DOWN THERE?"

From way down the hole something said, "Murmel, murmel, murmel."

"Hmmm," said Robin, "very strange." So she yelled, even louder, "ANYBODY DOWN THERE?"

"Murmel, murmel, murmel," said the hole. Robin reached down the hole as far as she could and gave an enormous yank. Out popped a baby.

"Murmel, murmel, murmel," said the baby.

"Murmel, yourself," said Robin. "I am only five years old and I can't take care of a baby. I will find somebody else to take care of you."

Robin picked up the very heavy baby and walked down the street. She met a woman pushing a baby carriage. Robin said, "Excuse me, do you need a baby?"

"Heavens, no," said the woman. "I already have a baby." She went off down the street and seventeen diaper salesmen jumped out from behind a hedge and ran after her.

Robin picked up the baby and went on down the street. She met an old woman and said, "Excuse me, do you need a baby?"

"Does it pee its pants?" said the old lady.

"Yes," said Robin.

"Yecch," said the old lady. "Does it dirty its diaper?"

"Yes," said Robin.

"Yecch," said the old lady. "Does it have a runny nose?"

"Yes," said Robin.

"Yecch," said the old lady. "I already have seventeen cats. I don't need a baby." She went off down the street. Seventeen cats jumped out of a garbage can and ran after her.

Robin picked up the baby and went down the street. She met a woman in fancy clothes. "Excuse me," said Robin, "do you need a baby?"

"Heavens, no," said the woman. "I have seventeen jobs, lots of money and no time. I don't need a baby." She went off down the street. Seventeen secretaries, nine messengers and a pizza delivery man ran after her.

"Rats," said Robin. She picked up the baby and walked down the street. She met a man. "Excuse me," she said, "do you need a baby?"

"I don't know," said the man. "Can it wash my car?"

"No," said Robin.

"Can I sell it for lots of money?"

"No," said Robin.

"Well, what is it for?" said the man.

"It is for loving and hugging and feeding and burping," said Robin.

"I certainly don't need that," said the man. He went off down the street. Nobody followed him.

Robin sat down beside the street, for the
baby was getting very heavy.

"Murmel, murmel, murmel," said the
baby.

"Murmel, yourself," said Robin. "What
am I going to do with you?"

An enormous truck came by and
stopped.

A truck driver jumped out and walked around Robin three times. Then he looked at the baby.

"Excuse me," said Robin, "do you need a baby?"

The truck driver said, "Weeeellll..."

"Murmel, murmel, murmel," said the baby.

"Did you say, 'murmel, murmel, murmel'?"asked the truck driver.

"Yes!" said the baby.

"I need you," yelled the truck driver. He picked up the baby and started walking down the street.

"Wait," said Robin, "you forgot your truck!"

"I already have seventeen trucks," said the truck driver. "What I need is a baby..."

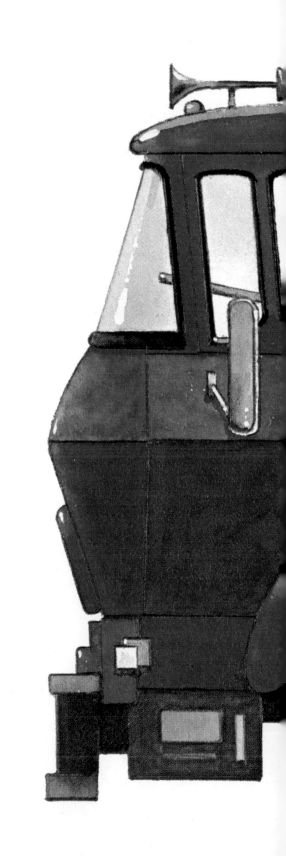

"YOU can have the truck."

Something Good

by Robert Munsch
illustrated by
Michael Martchenko

Tyya went shopping with her father and her brother and her sister. She pushed the cart up the aisle and down the aisle, up the aisle and down the aisle, up the aisle and down the aisle.

Tyya said, "Sometimes my father doesn't buy good food. He gets bread, eggs, milk, cheese, spinach—nothing any good! He doesn't buy ICE CREAM! COOKIES! CHOCOLATE BARS! or GINGER ALE!"

So Tyya very quietly snuck away from her father and got a cart of her own. She pushed it over to the ice cream. Then she put one hundred boxes of ice cream into her cart.

Tyya pushed that cart up behind her father and said, "DADDY, LOOK!" Her father turned around and yelled, "YIKES!"

Tyya said, "DADDY! GOOD FOOD!"

"Oh, no," said her father. "This is sugary junk. It will rot your teeth. It will lower your IQ. Put it ALL BACK!"

So Tyya put back the one hundred boxes of ice cream. She meant to go right back to her father, but on the way she had to pass the candy. She put three hundred chocolate bars into her cart.

Tyya pushed that cart up behind her father and said, "DADDY, LOOK!" Her father turned around and said, "YIKES!"

Tyya said, "DADDY! GOOD FOOD!"

"Oh, no," said her father. "This is sugary junk. Put it ALL BACK!" So Tyya put back all the chocolate bars. Then her father said, "Okay, Tyya, I have had it. You stand here and DON'T MOVE."

Tyya knew she was in BIG trouble, so she stood there and DIDN'T MOVE. Some friends came by and said hello. Tyya didn't move. A man ran over her toe with his cart. Tyya still didn't move.

A lady who worked at the store came by and looked at Tyya. She looked her over from the top down, and she looked her over from the bottom up. She knocked Tyya on the head—and Tyya still didn't move.

The lady said, "This is the nicest doll I have ever seen. It looks almost real." She put a price tag on Tyya's nose that said $29.95. Then she picked Tyya up and put her on the shelf with all the other dolls.

A man came along and looked at Tyya. He said, "This is the nicest doll I have ever seen. I'm going to get that doll for my son." He picked up Tyya by the hair.

Tyya yelled, very loudly, "STOP."

The man screamed, "EYAAAAH! IT'S ALIVE!" And he ran down the aisle, knocking over a pile of five hundred apples.

A lady came along and looked at Tyya. She said, "This is the nicest doll I have ever seen. I think I will buy this doll for my daughter." She picked up Tyya by the ear. Tyya yelled, as loudly as she could, "STOP."

The lady screamed, "EYAAAAH! IT'S ALIVE!" And she ran down the aisle, knocking over a pile of five hundred oranges.

Then Tyya's father came along, looking for his daughter. He said, "Tyya? Tyya? Tyya? Tyya? Where are you? ... TYYA! What are you doing on that shelf?"

Tyya said, "It's all your fault. You told me not to move and people are trying to buy me, WAAAAAHHHHH!"

"Oh, come now," said her father. "I won't let anybody buy you." He gave Tyya a big kiss and a big hug; then they went to pay for all the food.

The man at the cash register looked at Tyya and said, "Hey, Mister, you can't take that kid out of the store. You have to pay for her. It says so right on her nose: twenty-nine ninety-five."

"Wait," said the father. "This is my own kid. I don't have to pay for my own kid."

The man said, "If it has a price tag, you have to pay for it."

"I won't pay," said the father.

"You've got to," said the man.

The father said, "NNNNO."

The man said, "YYYYES."

The father said, "NNNNO!"

The man said, "YYYYES!"

The father and Andrew and Julie all yelled, "NNNNNNO!"

Then Tyya quietly said, "Daddy, don't you think I'm worth twenty-nine ninety-five?"

"Ah...Um...I mean... Well, of course you're worth twenty-nine ninety-five," said the father. He reached into his wallet, got out the money, paid the man, and took the price tag off Tyya's nose.

Tyya gave her father a big kiss, SMMMER-CCHH, and a big hug, MMMMMMMMMM, and then she said, "Daddy, you finally bought something good after all."

Then her father picked up Tyya and gave her a big long hug—and didn't say anything at all.

The Munsch for Kids series:

The Dark
Mud Puddle
The Paper Bag Princess
The Boy in the Drawer
Jonathan Cleaned Up, Then He Heard a Sound
Murmel Murmel Murmel
Millicent and the Wind
Mortimer
The Fire Station
Angela's Airplane
David's Father
Thomas' Snowsuit
50 Below Zero
I Have to Go!
Moira's Birthday
A Promise is a Promise
Pigs
Something Good
Show and Tell
Purple, Green and Yellow
Wait and See
Where is Gah-Ning?
From Far Away
Stephanie's Ponytail

Munschworks: The First Munsch Collection
Munschworks 3: The Third Munsch Treasury
Munschworks 4: The Fourth Munsch Treasury
The Munschworks Grand Treasury

Many Munsch titles are available in French and/or
Spanish. Please contact your favorite supplier.